Our Little Surprise

S.L. STERLING

S.L. Sterling

Our Little Surprise

ISBN: 978-1-989566-35-0

Paperback ISBN: 978-1-989566-36-7

Editor: Brandi Aquino, Editing Done Write

Cover Design: Thunderstruck Cover Design

Ainsley

It was a chilly day for the beginning of October, and the first few flakes of snow danced down in front of the window, immediately melting away as they hit the ground. I sat in the living room with my chin resting on my arm, looking out the front window of the house, trying to decide what I was going to do tonight. Normally, on Fridays, Dad would head over to the local pub to play pool with the guys from work, and I would sneak next door to Spencer's, but he was still away on a business trip until Monday. Perhaps I would call Carly. We hadn't hung out in a while. It would be nice to catch up, I thought to myself, glancing at the clock. I was about to reach for the phone when I turned back to look out the front window in time to see a car pull into Spencer's driveway. I leaned forward to see if I could see who it was. I could feel my excitement building at the thought of him returning early. I tried to lean forward a little more to see but the car had pulled up further than my view would allow and I hit my head on the window. I laughed at myself and then felt my phone vibrate in my pocket.

I quickly removed my phone from my front pocket and looked down at the screen to see a message waiting for me from RomanticAlpha42. A soft smile came to my lips as my body filled with excitement. Perhaps he had come home early, I thought to myself, and then glanced down the hall to make sure Dad wasn't coming and opened the message and read the words "I'm home" on my screen, and I quickly responded.

BabyGirl89: Dad is just getting ready to leave. I will be over as soon as he leaves.

RomanticAlpha42: Not tonight, tonight I'm coming to you. Let me know when the coast is clear. I want to destroy you in your bedroom this time.

I could barely contain myself as I giggled with excitement and squeezed my legs tight together at the thought of

Spencer between them after being gone for almost two weeks to set up the Denver office. We had spent an intense summer together, and this had been the first time we'd been apart for any amount of time. I shoved my phone back into my pocket when I heard my father clear his throat. "What are you so happy about?" he questioned.

"It's nothing," I said, shaking my head. "You look nice." I looked at my father. He wore dark dress pants, a shirt, and tie. It was odd to see my father in anything but jeans and a T-shirt, but it suited him, and besides, I needed to do whatever it took to take the focus off me.

"Thanks, I have a date tonight."

"Oh, I thought you were going to meet up with your work buddies at the bar."

"Not tonight."

“So who is the date with?"

"You don't know her. I met her through Spencer's company. That man was right. I don't know why I waited so long to join Finding Forever."

"Will you be out late?" I questioned as my father stepped in front of the mirror to straighten his tie. I watched him try to adjust it, and then he turned to me, a look of despair on his face at the fact his tie was still crooked.

"Who knows?" he said, laughing. "I will not rush it. I am going to adopt Spencer's rule. Whatever happens,

happens. So don't you wait up," Dad said, raising his eyebrows.

I couldn't help but giggle. I was happy for my father. After years of being single and focusing all his time on raising me after my mom left us, he was finally getting out there. It had taken Spencer a long time to convince my father to finally use his company.

Finding Forever was an elite matchmaking site. It wasn't one of those sign up and get laid sites as Spencer would call them. This one was meant to find you a forever relationship. He had spent years marketing the company, acquiring the right clients, and it had paid off. Even though my father said he didn't want a forever relationship, I knew deep down inside he did.

"Well, Dad, have a great time okay."

"I will. Oh and how are things going at work? I meant to ask you the other day, but it slipped my mind. Is Spencer still treating you okay?"

I felt a slight blush hit my cheeks at Dad's question. Spencer was treating me more than okay. I'd had a crush on that man for months, and after finding what I was sure was his handle on Finding Forever in a magazine ad, I'd created a fake profile and began messaging him. My friend Carly disapproved immediately, and I was convinced there was no way he would use his real handle on a magazine ad anyways. Soon, I found myself messaging with this person almost daily, and then one night while I was babysitting for him, he'd come home late and offered me a glass of wine. I'd been texting with RomanticAlpha42 most of the night, but when I'd accepted to stay for the drink, I sent him a quick text and Spencer's phone went off.

At first, I thought it was a coincidence, so I sent another one. However, when I heard his phone go off again, I panicked. I raced to leave, but he didn't give me a chance, and soon I was under him. We'd agreed to keep our relationship secret. After all, he was my dad's best friend.

I'd started working at Finding Forever. Spencer's executive assistant had transferred to a new location, and I had just graduated from college. It was a job I loved, and it gave us permission to fool around after hours, of course, with no interruption from my father, his ex-wife, or Nikki, his seven-year-old daughter.

I cleared my throat. "Things are going great," I answered, straightening the tie Dad was wearing.

Dad turned and looked in the mirror, impressed with my tie straightening skills. "Wow, where on earth did you learn to do that?" he asked, knowing full well I'd never held a serious relationship before.

Truth was I had come to learn to straighten ties almost immediately after Spencer and I had had an intense session of hot sex against his office wall.

I shrugged. "It's just easier when someone else does it," I said, turning away from my father.

"When is Spencer supposed to be back from that business trip?"

"Um, I believe he said Monday. At least that was what his schedule said. Why?"

"Good, I have to go out of town for work on Monday. I feel better knowing he is home next door to look over you when I am gone."

I felt a blush rise to my cheeks and hoped that my father hadn't seen it. He wouldn't feel better if he knew that Spencer and I were involved. He certainly wouldn't feel better if he knew the things Spencer and I had done together when he'd been gone.

"What time are you supposed to be meeting this woman?" I asked, feeling my phone vibrate in my pocket.

"I pick her up in ten minutes. I guess I should probably get going. She lives on the other side of town," he said, looking at his watch.

I handed Dad his jacket and practically shoved him out the door and watched as he ran down the front steps of the house. "Make sure you keep the doors locked, and if you're feeling ambitious, why don't you pull up some of the Christmas decorations from the basement," He called out as he climbed in the car.

"I might," I yelled. I waved just as he pulled out of the

driveway and watched until he was out of sight, then I took my phone and sent Spencer a message.

BabyGirl89: He's gone.

Spencer didn't respond. Instead, in a matter of minutes, he was standing in the entryway of the house, and I was pressed up against the wall in his embrace with his lips tightly pressed to mine.

"Oh God, Ainsley, how I missed this," Spencer gritted out. My hand was wrapped around his cock, gently stroking him, as he ran his tongue through my wet center.

I let out a loud moan as he concentrated on the little bundle of nerves, first licking then gently sucking it into his mouth.

"Did you miss this?" he asked as he slid two fingers inside of me, curling them to hit that special spot inside me as he sucked my clit into his mouth again.

I arched my back up off the bed. I was ready to explode, but I knew if I said anything, Spencer would stop and wait for me to come back down.

"So much," I raggedly whispered, completely breathless.

"You ready for more?" he questioned, running his fingers lightly over the inside of my thighs, placing gentle kisses where his fingers had just traveled.

"Please," I begged as I arched my back off the mattress. "Give me more."

I heard his low, throaty chuckle, and then he knelt before me, gripped my ankles, and rested my legs on his shoulders, gripping my hips tightly as he slowly sunk himself into me. I cried out as he started to pump deep and slow inside of me.

He reached down between us, and with every pump, he ran his thumb over that small bundle, driving me crazy. I didn't say anything as I gripped his wrist, he already knew I was willing him to stop, begging him to stop, but he didn't listen.

"No way, baby girl," he whispered as my climax continued to grow until I couldn't hold back anymore. I screamed out his name as I tightened around him. He held me tight, his breathing became more and more ragged, he pumped harder, faster, and deeper inside of me until he had emptied himself inside of me and collapsed against me, breathing hard.

A little while later, I lay in Spencer's arms, my head against his strong chest with my eyes closed while he ran his fingers lightly along my arm, placing gentle kisses on the top of my shoulder. "I love you, Ainsley," Spencer whispered.

I swallowed hard at his confession. I'd been dying to hear him say those words. I had been dying to say them to him but figured he would think it was just me being a naive little girl. Instead, he had said it first, and yet as the words rolled off his lips, a funny feeling sat in the pit of my stomach.

It took me a moment, but I swallowed hard and then whispered, "I love you too."

He rolled me onto my back and kissed me hard, then he pulled me into his arms.

"I really should get home," he said, kissing my neck. “I have a pile of paperwork to get through plus I don’t want to run into your father.”

"Just stay a little while longer. I've missed laying in your arms," I pleaded, placing small kisses along his neck. I hadn’t realized how much I had missed it until I felt them around me again.

"All right. I wanted to talk to you about something anyways.”

I could see the troubled look on his face and I was worried that something was wrong. “What is it?”

“I think it’s time we speak with your father, tell him the truth about what has been going on between us."

I swallowed hard. I'd been thinking about that as well and knew that if things between us continued to get serious then we'd have no choice. "Can we wait until after Christmas?"

Spencer shook his head. "I think we should tell him before. I'd really like to be able to have you spend nights with me without sneaking around behind your father's back."

"What about Brittany?"

"We'll tell her too. It probably won't go over well but I don't want to hide anymore. Nikki will be thrilled. She loves you. I love you."

I met Spencer's eyes and, even though I was unsure. "It will be fine. I promise," he whispered, placing his hand against my cheek and bringing his lips to mine in a deep, firm kiss.

I had no idea how or when we had drifted off, but when I opened my eyes, my room was dark. At first, I had thought Spencer's return had only been a dream, but when I went to move, I realized I was spooned in Spencer's arms.

I went to move but stopped. My body ached in places that fully reminded me of what had happened only a few hours before. Then his words came rushing back to me. He loved me. He wanted to tell my father and his ex-wife that we were together. Again, anticipation and nerves filled me, and I softly smiled to myself as I allowed the excitement of not having to sneak around fill me. I adjusted the covers so I could roll over and bury my face in his chest like I normally did when we'd spend the night together. Only instead of snuggling down, I froze. A dark figure standing just inside my bedroom door caught my eye, and the excitement I'd felt only seconds ago was replaced with alarm. I now remembered what had woken me—a noise, the click of my bedroom door when my father had opened it. Our eyes locked in the darkness. I could already see the look of shock, anger, and disappointment flooding his face.

I didn't know what to do as panic continued to fill me, and I froze. We'd been caught. We'd been doing this for months and we'd been so careful. Each of us always having an alibi every single time we'd been together, until now. Spencer had decided for the first time to come to me instead of me going to him and now we'd been caught.

"What in the actual fuck is going on here?" my father roared and turned on the bedroom light.

Spencer jumped, covering his eyes from the bright overhead light for a moment, and then he looked around the room, his eyes wide as he looked at my father.

"Daddy, please don't get angry," I pleaded. "Let me explain." I cried, pulling the covers up over my naked body.

My father looked at Spencer, and he shook his head. "I fucking trusted you with her, you son of a bitch."

"Jon, calm down. It's not what it looks like," Spencer said, trying to keep a level head.

My father let out this maniacal laughter I'd never heard before. "You can tell her that—she's a fucking child—but you sure as hell can't tell me that. This is exactly what it looks like. I'm giving you five minutes to get the fuck out of my house."

"Dad, I'm a grown woman. I'll do what I want!" I shouted.

"Ainsley, I don't want to hear it right now. Spencer, five fucking minutes, not a damn second longer. I don't want to see you around her again, you got it."

With tears streaming down my face, my father turned and slammed my bedroom door shut. I looked at Spencer, who threw the covers off himself, swearing under his breath, slid into his jeans. He came over to me, wrapping me tightly in his strong arms, pulling me against the warmth of his chest as I sobbed.

"This will blow over. When he isn't so mad, I'll talk to him, okay. Just like we talked about," he whispered, pressing his lips to mine. "I'll explain everything. It will be okay. Send me a message in the morning."

I nodded, trying hard to stifle the sobs, but it did little good as I watched him grab his shirt. He threw it over his head and ran his fingers through his messed-up hair. Then he turned back to me and kissed me one final time and opened my bedroom door and stepped out into the hall, closing it behind him. He hadn't been gone a minute when I heard elevated voices in the hallway. I climbed off my bed, threw my robe on, and opened the door to find my father and Spencer in an intense, heated conversation.

"You're not to see her anymore, you understand me. She isn't going to be babysitting for Nikki neither, and I want her to resign immediately from Finding Forever."

Spencer was about to say something, but I didn't give him the chance.

"No!" I screamed. "I will still babysit, and I'm not quitting my job."

"The fuck you will. You live under my roof. You'll do as I say. As for you, Spencer, our friendship is over. Now get the fuck out of here."

"I'm going with him," I said, taking a step forward, but my father stopped me, gripping my upper arms tightly.

"Get to bed," he gritted.

Tears welled in my eyes as my father pushed me back toward my bedroom. I tried to see around him, but he blocked my view from seeing Spencer turn and walked out the front door. I heard it click shut, and I stood in the hallway glaring at my father.

"When you return to work after your vacation, you resign, you hear me?" he said, looking into my eyes.

"Dad, you aren't being fair. Spencer and I—"

Dad held his hand up to my face to stop me from speaking. "Those are two words I don't ever want to hear used in the same sentence again. I'm so disappointed in you, Ainsley. In both of you. Now go to bed," he gritted as he walked by me, slamming his bedroom door shut.

I stood in the dark hallway wondering if I should just sneak out and go to Spencer. I felt empty inside, and I wanted to be comforted by him, but then I heard my dad banging around in his bedroom and thought twice. Spencer was right; it would blow over after he explained everything. I just needed to give him the chance.

Ainsley

It had been two weeks since the mishap, and my father hadn't let me out of his sight. I looked over at the pile of boxes he had pulled up from the basement marked Christmas and let out a sigh as I looked down at my plate of breakfast my stomach feeling uneasy. In the past two weeks I had barely gotten out of bed or eaten anything since the night my father found us.

I had watched from my window as Spencer tried to talk to my father over the backyard fence as Dad was raking up the leaves, getting everything ready for winter. Even with my window open, I couldn't hear what was being said, but what I could see was the look on my father's face. A look I'd grown accustomed to over the last little while. He wasn't planning to listen to anything Spencer had to say.

I sat there swirling my fork through my already cold eggs, watching the screen of my phone for a message from Spencer, but my phone was silent and had been since eight last night. I knew that Spencer's ex-wife was coming to drop Nikki off for the weekend, so I figured that perhaps he was busy with that, or I hoped that was the reason why I hadn't heard from him.

I blew out a frustrated breath as Dad walked into the kitchen.

"I spoke to Brittany," he said as he reached for his lunch bag.

"You what?" I gritted, gripping my fork tight in my hand. "You had no right to talk to her."

Immediately, I wanted to pick up my phone and warn Spencer before she got there, but my dad stood there watching me, leaning against the counter sipping his coffee. Brittany was miserable at the best of times. I could just imagine what her reaction would be to this news.

"My ruling stands: no more babysitting, no more being around him when you are unsupervised. I have no idea how long the two of you have been sneaking around behind my back, but I am sure it's been a while."

"Why on earth would you have spoken to Brittany?" I questioned. "Besides, it's not like that."

"Really, what's it like then?"

I slammed my fork down on the table. I was tired of listening to it. It had been utter hell at home since Dad had found us, and it got worse every single time Spencer tried to talk to him.

I'd snuck out of the house yesterday when Dad had gone to a work meeting and met Spencer for coffee. He assured me he had tried to talk to him, but every time he would bring up the subject of us with my father, he would immediately shut the conversation down.

"Dad, I can assure you this was all very consensual. He didn't force himself on me."

"Ainsley, please, I should have the man charged. He's taking advantage of you."

I shook my head. "No, Dad, he isn't. We are in love."

My father threw his lunch into his bag and let out a laugh. "Ainsley, your inexperience wouldn't allow you to see it. You're impressionable, and I can assure you that he is taking advantage of you. Besides, you wouldn't know what love is. You're just a kid. Now, I have to go to work."

"I'm an adult, Dad," I mumbled under my breath. "Why would you have spoken to Brittany?" I murmured, placing my face in my hands, my stomach rolling at the thought that she was going to ambush Spencer this morning without warning.

"Well, to be honest, I felt it was only fair that she knew what was going on behind closed doors when her daughter was involved."

Spencer and his ex-wife weren't on the best of terms. They had never been on the best of terms, and I could only imagine what her finding out this information may do. I glared at my father, "I hate you," I spat.

"Good, hate me. That's fine. One day when you realize what this really is, you will thank me."

"Dad, you're not being fair. Be angry at us, hate Spencer but you didn't have to say anything to Brittany."

"Oh, but I did. Her daughter spends weekends there and you spend nights there when you babysit. That means shit has been going on while she is there, and since you are an adult, as you put it, I hope you're prepared because she was angry."

I could feel the anger boiling over inside of me as I watched Dad grab his bag off the counter and walked out the back door. I looked down at my breakfast, my stomach turning, saliva flooding my mouth. I picked up my plate and carried it to the garbage, dumping the contents, and placed the plate in the sink when I heard the back door open. Dad walked back in and looked at me. I turned my back on him and looked out the back window.

"Ainsley, I forgot, make sure you prepare your resignation letter today. I want to see it before you hand to Spencer when you return to work on Monday. I know he will be expecting it."

I balled my fists tight, jumping as the back door slammed. I stood there staring down at the mess of egg yolk all over my plate and buried my face in my hands, trying hard to fight back the tears. I pulled my phone from my pocket. I was about to message Spencer to see if we could meet for lunch, but there was already a message waiting for me telling me to call him as soon as I had a minute.

I looked out the back door to make sure my father was gone then quickly dialed his number. I'd hoped that he still had a few more hours alone. I needed him.

"Spencer Brooks," his sexy, deep voice came over the phone, instantly calming me.

"It's me," I said, doing my best to sound happy, even though every aspect of my life was in turmoil.

"One second," he said.

I waited, listening to the noise in the background, and knew he was in the office. "Sorry, had to shut the door."

"That's okay."

"Listen, I would prefer to talk to you in person, but since that isn't possible right now, this will have to do."

"I can meet you somewhere," I said. "Or I can come to the office."

"No, it's fine." His voice cracked, then he went quiet.

I knew something was wrong just by the sound of his voice. I took in a deep breath, "What is it?" I asked, alarm filling my chest.

"Ainsley, Brittany found out somehow what has been going on between us."

"Yeah, about that. Apparently, my father called and spoke with her," I bit out, worried at what he was going to say next. "He said he felt she should know what was going on between us. I don't know why my dad just can't stay out of it."

The phone was silent. I could barely even hear Spencer breathing on the other end. I was beginning to think he had hung up so I just said what came to my mind. "I tried to tell him everything was consensual and that we were in love—"

"She's threatened to take Nikki from me, Ainsley," Spencer interjected.

It felt as if all the air had been sucked out of the room, and if I thought I was going to be sick before I was really going to be sick now as the room started to spin. I knew how much Nikki meant to Spencer, and I knew that something like this would devastate him if she actually went through with it. "Can she do that? I mean..."

"Yes. If she deems my place to be unsafe place, and that I'm irresponsible, all she needs to do is call her lawyer. They will investigate and it will be over. Ainsley, I can't lose Nikki."

"I'm sorry, Spencer. I hate my father right now."

"I'm sorry, too, Ainsley." His voice shook, "I think it might be best if for the time being we just go our separate ways until things cool off."

My hand immediately covered my mouth and tears spilled down my cheeks. I could barely breathe as Spencer continued talking, and the lump that sat in my throat hurt like hell. It was only a few more minutes before he had finished saying all he needed to say and then I heard him utter good-bye. I sunk to the kitchen floor, my feet unable to hold me, as my heart broke.

"How was your massage?" Carly asked as she took a sip of her cucumber water.

"Fine." I sat down in the lounge chair beside Carly, leaned back, closed my eyes, and let out a huge sigh. My entire body ached from all the stress I'd been dealing with over the last couple weeks.

"I know you think your life is over, but could you at least act as if you are enjoying yourself?" Carly said, looking over at me with a worried expression on her face.

"Please, just stop. You have no idea what I'm going through."

"I do. I have been involved with someone before you know."

"It's not the same. You really have no idea, Carly. I'm so mad at my dad right now. He has made my life hell."

"No, he didn't, you did that. I told you not to get involved with Spencer. I told you right from the start this whole ordeal would end with nothing but trouble, but you refused to listen."

I rolled my eyes. I was so tired of listening to her go on about this. I met her eyes, which gleamed nothing but 'I told you so.' "Please, for once, can you just be on my side, please."

Carly grabbed her robe and swung her legs over the side so she could sit up. "Look, I'm sorry. I feel bad for you, I really do. I just..."

"I know you just feel that I am getting what I deserve. You told me so, I know."

Carly's face fell at my words. I knew I wasn't being fair to her, but I was tired of my best friend not taking how I felt into consideration. I leaned my head back against the lounge chair and closed my eyes, trying to find something other than my troubles to talk about.

"What are you going to do about the job?"

I blew out a breath and looked out the sunroom windows at the lake. "I don't want to quit, but that is what my dad wants, and I am sure Brittany will be urging Spencer to let me go. So, my father will get his way in some regard. I will probably just put in a transfer. I do like working there, it's good money, and Christmas is right around the corner."

"Might be for the best. I'm glad to see that you are making the right decision in that regard."

"What is that supposed to mean?" I exclaimed, sitting up and looking at Carly, ready for a fight.

"Nothing. We should get changed and head down for lunch."

I watched Carly as she stood up, avoiding eye contact with me. I knew there was some meaning behind her comment. I just didn't know what it was in this moment. "I'll be along in a minute," I whispered as Carly got up and made her way toward the changing room.

Once Carly left the room, I leaned back on the lounge chair I was sitting on and tried to think everything through. I had been the one to start all of this. I had lit the fire, and now I was the one who was getting burned.

I picked up my cell phone and checked it for messages, praying there was one from Spencer telling me that he was sorry and had made a mistake, but there was nothing more from him. I took a minute and started composing a message to him, but halfway through, something stopped me and I deleted it. I had to let him go, I just needed to figure out how to do it.

Spencer

I sat across from my ex-wife. She sat there with a scowl on her face, her arms crossed over her chest as she glared at me. The tension in the room could have been cut with a knife. It seriously felt like our divorce proceedings all over again. I drummed my fingers on the table, more to annoy her than anything. She had come to pick Nikki up my weekend with her, and she looked even more miserable now than she did when she dropped her off.

"I swear, Spencer, she better not have been here this weekend. You know Nikki will tell me if she was so you're better off to spill it now."

"For fuck sakes, Brittany, how many times do I have to tell you, she wasn't here. Nikki and I went to see some Christmas lights, and then to the toy store so she could pick out some toys that she wants for Christmas."

"You're lying, just give it up already, I've already called my lawyer. He thinks I should pursue for full custody."

I chuckled. "Of course, he does." I muttered.

"What is that supposed to mean?"

I glared at her, leaning forward, "Should we go down the path of what really led to our divorce? Not to mention the shit that goes on in your home now?"

"What is that supposed to mean?"

"How quickly you forget." I looked down at my phone to see what date it was. Yep, exactly two weeks from today. "November 15th, I returned from a business trip from our Florida office. The house was dark. Figuring you were in bed, I ran up the stairs, checked in on Nikki, who was sound asleep, and then made my way down to our bedroom. I opened the door and heard the shower running. The door was partially open, and so I decide that I'd surprise you in the shower. Only the surprise was on me because, instead of finding you alone in there, I find you wrapped in the arms of another man as he is fucking you up against the shower wall," I said, elevating my voice.

Brittany looked at me shocked. She hadn't known I had walked in on her and witnessed that. She thought the coast had been clear because I had gotten dressed, left the house, and sat at the end of the street in my car until I had seen him leave.

"Keep your voice down," she bit out in a whisper. "How did you know about that?"

"For fuck sakes, Brit, I just told you, because I walked in and found the two of you. Instead of pulling him out of the shower and killing him, like I should have, I realized that was why you had been so withdrawn out of our relationship. You'd been seeing him behind my back for God knows how long. If you really want to draw this all out in court again, I'll make sure the judge knows not only about that, but about the other slew of men you bring home on a weekly basis."

"I don't," she said, crossing her arms.

"Really? Nikki sure seems to mention them. Paul, Sebastian, Cody, oh and my personal favorite, Axel. If you'd like, I can bring her down here and ask her about them."

Brittany let out a huff. "Nikki, honey, you almost ready to go," she yelled to our daughter.

"As always, run when things get tough."

"You're screwing your fucking babysitter," she said, turning her wild eyes on me. "The child you decided to put in charge of my daughter's well-being when you are away. At least the men I'm involved with are grown adults."

"I seriously doubt that and Ainsley is not a child."

Nikki came down the hall dragging her tiny pink suitcase behind her, carrying her favorite teddy bear under her arm. "Daddy, will Ainsley be watching me next time I'm here. I miss her. She always plays games with me too. I made her this," Nikki said, walking over to me and dropping a pink bracelet into the palm of my hand. "I think she will love it. She said she wanted one just like mine. I even made a card," Nikki said, handing me a pink piece of construction paper with a picture she had drawn on the front.

Brittany let out a loud huff and stood up. "Wonderful," she bit out under her breath.

"I'll make sure I give it to her."

"I'm sure you will," Brittany bit out.

I gave her a nasty look and turned my attention back to my daughter.

My chest felt empty at the thought of possibly never being able to hold Nikki in my arms again. I took the bracelet from her and placed a kiss on the top of Nikki's head then placed my hand on her back and walked her to the door where I helped put her little shoes on.

"Take your bag to the car, Nikki. I'll be out in a minute," Brittany said.

Nikki turned and looked up at me. "Daddy, when I come back can we get the Christmas tree. I want to pick it out, but maybe Ainsley can come with us. She loves hot chocolate with marshmallows, remember. I will save my allowance and buy her one," Nikki said, jumping up and down, waiting for me to say yes.

"I'll think about it, okay. Now do as your mom says and take your bag out to the car."

"Okay," she said with a pout as I bent to kiss the top of her head.

As soon as Nikki was out of earshot, Brittany turned back to me. "Look, I won't pursue full custody until after Christmas, but I swear to God, Spencer, if I find out that child is back in this house looking after our daughter, I will change my mind. It would be a sad Christmas for Nikki if she couldn't see you," she threatened and threw her purse over her shoulder and marched down the front steps of the house. I watched as she got Nikki into the car and then pulled out of the driveway.

The instant I shut the door, anger filled me and I went over to the phone and called my lawyer just to be on the safe side, leaving him a message to fill him in on what was going on. Then I grabbed a glass from the cupboard and poured myself a scotch, dropping two ice cubes into the golden liquid. I downed the first glass, relishing in the burn, then poured another glass and went to watch the news.

That night, as I lay in bed with my arms behind my head, my thoughts traveled to Ainsley. How I missed going to sleep with her lying in my arms. I thought about the call we'd had prior to Nikki arriving on the weekend. I had been wrong to tell her that I wanted to end things. I had strictly done it out of fear.

I reached over to my night table and grabbed my phone, opening our chat. I had typed out a full-on apology, and then something inside of me decided against sending it. I wasn't going to do this through a text. I'd wait and talk to her tomorrow morning the second she arrived at the office, and we would work everything out.

Ainsley

The lobby of Finding Forever looked amazing all decorated up for Christmas. I greeted a couple of girls who sat behind the reception desk and then walked over to the elevator. My nerves were uneasy. I had spent the entire weekend sulking, wishing that my father hadn't spoken to Brittany, and then wishing Spencer would message me, but when I didn't hear from him by the time I'd gone to bed, I had finally concluded that perhaps I really didn't know what was going on between us. As much as I didn't want to say everyone else was right, perhaps they were, and so I had gotten out of bed at one in the morning and filled out a transfer form.

The ride to the top floor didn't seem to take as long as it normally did, and when the doors opened, I stepped off the elevator, manila envelope in hand, and walked over to my desk. My stomach was in knots as I placed my coat on a hook in the corner of my space and shoved my purse into the bottom drawer of my desk. I saw that Spencer's door was already closed, which meant he had arrived early and was probably in a meeting. Again, doubt filled my mind, and I seriously thought of just shoving that envelope into the back of one of my desk drawers and forgetting about it. Instead, I sat down and turned on my computer and quickly checked his calendar to see if he was indeed in the middle of a meeting before going and knocking on his door. His calendar this morning was clear, which made my stomach flop yet again. I took a deep breath, grabbed the envelope off my desk, and knocked on his office door.

"Come in," I heard him say in that deep, business-like voice I'd grown used to.

I closed my eyes, composed myself, and opened the door. He was focused on something as he sat behind his desk looking as handsome as ever. His suit jacket hung on the back of his chair. The sleeves of his white dress shirt were rolled up, exposing his strong forearms. He wore no tie today, his shirt open at the neck, and immediately my thoughts went to kissing that soft spot where his neck met the top of his shoulder. I swallowed hard as I caught the scent of his cologne. He looked up from his paperwork, his eyes running over my body, and smiled.

"Good morning. Come in, shut the door. I have something I'd like to discuss with you."

I froze, unsure of what I should do. Instead, I didn't close the door I stepped forward. "I have something I would like to discuss with you. I'd like to go first," I said and held out the envelope for him to take. "Here."

Spencer looked at me, the smile he had on his face quickly vanishing. "What's this?" he questioned, taking it from me and opening it.

"I'm putting in a transfer." I swallowed hard, even though I felt this was wrong from the time I'd filled it out last night, but yet I somehow knew it was the right thing to do, especially after Spencer told me that Brittany could take Nikki from him. I didn't want the man to lose his little girl. I loved her as much as I loved him.

He sat there looking over the page, then he set it down on his desk and crossed his arms in front of him. "Are you not happy here?"

"No, I am. Dad wanted me to resign but I figured this was a better option. I just really need you to sign that, please. There is an opening in the finance department, and I would like to take that position."

Spencer looked down at the sheet again and then back up to me. "I didn't know you took any interest in finance."

I shrugged. I didn't take interest in finance and there was no way I was going to pretend that I did, but there were no other openings at this time. I looked to the floor and back up to him. "I'm, um, expanding my horizons."

Spencer sat back in his chair and chuckled, then shook

his head. "You know, I appreciate people who aren't afraid to better themselves, but in this case, I'm sorry, I won't sign it."

My eyes flew open. "You won't sign it? What do you mean you won't sign it?"

"I mean, no. With everything coming up over the holidays, I am going to need you here. So, I am not signing this," he said, picking up my transfer sheet and setting it off to the far side of his desk.

"You can't do that. I mean, you have to sign it."

He chuckled. "Ainsley, I can do whatever I want. I own the company, remember? And I must do what is best for the interest of the company. We have our Christmas party in less than a month, and I am going to need your help to finish organizing it. If I were to sign this, I would need to hire and train a new assistant. You and I both know that will take months, and there would be no way that they could organize a function of this magnitude on such short notice."

"Spencer, that's not my problem. That is yours. Besides, you haven't even mentioned a Christmas party for your clients. Now, please sign the transfer."

"I haven't mentioned it to you because I was away for the last two weeks, but I was planning to talk to you today about it. Now if you'd care to get your notepad and pen we can start getting things down for this function."

I looked at Spencer, highly annoyed, first at the fact he

wouldn't sign my transfer and now at the fact that he was assuming I would just bend over and organize this party. "I'm sorry, but I really don't think I am capable of organizing this function either. I have worked for this company for a few months, and besides, I have no experience in the event planning area, so I think you really should talk to the events department."

Spencer chuckled. "Well, you have no experience in finance either, yet you wish to transfer to that department."

I could feel my blood pressure rising as he sat there with a cocky grin on his face.

"I can learn," I gritted.

"Well then you can learn how to organize this event then. Colleen was working on it, but she is out of the office. She had surgery a week ago and will be off until January, maybe February. So, I'm left with no choice. We will work together to organize it, and you can learn."

I looked at Spencer and then glanced around his office, my eyes landing back on my transfer form that sat on his desk unsigned. This had totally blown up in my face. Not only did I do this so Spencer wouldn't lose Nikki, I had done it so that I wouldn't hear my father lecturing me on the fact he wanted me to resign. He would not be happy to know that instead I'd now be working in close quarters with Spencer. "I'll make you a deal."

"All right." He nodded. "What's the deal?"

"I'll help you organize this event and see you through the holidays on the condition that in the new year you sign my transfer form."

Spencer studied my face and nodded. "If that is what you really want."

I thought for a moment. It wasn't what I wanted at all. As I looked into his eyes, I knew that what I really wanted was to be back in his arms, but I knew that wasn't possible either. I looked down at the floor and then back up to Spencer. "It's what I want."

Spencer held out his large hand for me to take, but when I hesitated, he asked, "What is it?"

"It's just, if we are going to plan this party together, then it needs to be kept on a professional level."

Spencer looked at me, that cocky grin coming to his lips. "Are you suggesting that I don't know how to work with a woman on a professional level?"

His eyes danced with a look I knew all too well, and I had to bite my bottom lip to hide my smile. "I didn't say that. I just wanted to remind you."

Spencer looked at me and held out his hand again. I slipped mine into his and, as soon as we touched, a shock ran through my body. "Now, go get your notepad."

Dad was sitting in his favorite chair watching TV when I got home. I dropped my purse by the back door and slipped my shoes off and then walked into the living room and flopped down into the chair.

"You're home late," he said, turning to me.

"I had a lot of work to do today."

"You put your resignation in?" he questioned, throwing a handful of nuts into his mouth and washing them down with a swig of beer.

I knew he was going to start this. I shook my head.

"Ainsley, we talked about this," he said, slamming his bottle down on the table.

"Relax, I put a transfer in. There is no need for me to quit a perfectly fine paying job, especially with Christmas around the corner."

"All right, when do you start in the new position?"

My stomach filled with nerves as he continued to pay attention to me instead of the fishing show he was watching. I wasn't sure what to tell him. I wasn't sure I wanted to tell him.

"Ainsley?"

"After Christmas," I murmured.

"That is over six weeks away. There is no way you are going to be working with this man that long. I fucking told him," Dad barked reaching for his cell phone.

"Dad. It's fine. He needs help to plan the annual Christmas party. The woman in charge of events is off on surgery, and a new person couldn't look after something like this. His hands were tied."

Dad looked at me skeptically. "Ainsley, you have no experience planning anything like that. I don't like this. He's doing this on purpose." I watched as he began to type.

"And I have no experience in the finance department either," I bit out. "Yet I put a transfer in."

Dad looked over the rim of his glasses at me. "Well you can learn," he said, going right back to whatever message he was planning on sending to Spencer.

"Yep, I can. I can also learn how to plan an event. Spencer promised to keep everything strictly professional, and after the holidays he told me he would sign my transfer."

Dad stopped typing. "You know I'll talk to him and make sure, so you better be telling me the truth."

"I am. I promise." I said and watched as he placed his phone down on the table and turned his attention back to the TV.

Spencer

Ainsley and I had worked diligently over the last two weeks getting all the details down for the Christmas party. I'd behaved myself as promised, working only in a professional manner, a far cry from what we were before, a far cry from where I'd hoped we be by now once again. I missed those moments where our hands touched and our eyes locked. I missed the secret looks we shared in front of other employees, I missed taking her on my desk when we worked late, but most of all, I missed those nights that I held her tenderly in my arms.

I'd searched my soul for a long time after Brittany had left me, always afraid to allow myself to get close to someone, afraid to fall in love with someone for fear of getting hurt. The first time I allowed it, I fell in deep, and now I'm forbidden to be with her, not only by my ex-wife but by her father, the second of which I can honestly say I understand.

I'd spent the last little bit doing more soul searching, and something felt different this morning as I watched her walk into the office. I don't know if it was the fact that I was tired of allowing someone else to dictate to me how I was supposed to feel or what. I'd spent the past twenty years of my life making others happy, while the last eight I'd been miserable, except for the past few months with Ainsley. That alone resonated so loudly with me, and I wasn't having it anymore.

I'd called Ainsley into my office more than usual today, pretending that I couldn't find something on a spreadsheet just so that I could feel her heat beside me. She looked amazing in the tight white sweater dress she wore. She stood beside me showing me what I had been looking for and then walked around to the other side of my desk and stood there.

I couldn't help but allow myself to look at her. She was amazingly sexy, and when my eyes met hers, I could tell from the look on her face that I had allowed my eyes to linger on her longer than was appropriate given our situation. Instead of saying anything, she looked at me and softly smiled, then turned and left my office. I knew in that moment that she still felt the same way about me as I did about her. Now I just needed to show her.

It was a little after seven, a storm raged on outside, and I dimmed the overhead lights in my office and turned on the three smaller lamps that were scattered around. Then I poked my head out the door. Ainsley was sitting at her desk, phone to her ear, making notes, while discussing the menu for the party. I partially shut my door and went online and ordered food and wine from The Herbed Oyster for delivery. Then I quickly scribbled 'food is on the way' on a Post-it.

I casually walked over to her desk, dropping the note down on the pad of paper in front of her, and continued on my way to the washroom. When I glanced back, I saw her read the note and she raised her eyes to mine. I chuckled as I heard her ask the woman to repeat herself.

She was still deep in conversation when I returned, so I made my way into the office and sat down behind my desk, clearing everything out of the way. I had just finished when the delivery man knocked on my door.

. . .

"Sir, you ordered food?" he asked.

"Yes, please come in. You may set it right here," I said, pointing to the cleared space on my desk.

He did as I asked as I pulled the money from my wallet. Once he was gone, I quickly arranged the plate of oysters and poured two glasses of Chablis.

"How about you just email me the menu and I will look it over and confirm with you tomorrow," I heard Ainsley say. "That way if I need to make any changes I can."

I laid out a couple other dishes I had ordered, and then I stepped out into the hall just in time to see Ainsley gathering up the notes she had made, placing them in the event folder.

"The menu should be finalized tomorrow morning, and as soon as you've approved it, I'll confirm and book the caterer. Oh and she said she won't need final guest numbers until a week prior, which is good because two days prior to her due date is when we had set the RSVP cut-off date."

I didn't respond. Instead, I leaned up against the wall and looked over at her. She was adorable as she stood there all business like struggling to get the folder into her bag.

She looked up, probably expecting me not to be there, since I had not responded, and locked eyes with me. "What? What is it?" she asked.

"I ordered in a little late-night snack. Why don't you come join me?"

She looked around at her desk and then nervously down at her watch. "Um. I really should be getting home. It's getting late."

"Ainsley, it's a little after seven thirty. This is nothing more than a simple bite to eat between friends. A little thank you for all the work you've been doing. Nothing more," I said, disappointed that she hadn't jumped at the chance like she used to.

She looked around at the quiet office and nodded. "You're right. I am a little hungry actually." She put the folder down on her desk and went to slip her shoes on.

"There's no need to put shoes on. It's after hours, you can be comfortable," I said, nodding to the heels she was about to slip on.

She stopped and looked down at her shoes, her brow furrowed, and then she walked into my office. I closed the door behind us, giving us privacy from the cleaning crew that would be arriving any moment. I walked over and picked up the two glasses of wine, handing her one.

"To another successful day of planning," I said, raising my glass to hers.

. . .

She hesitated at first, and then she took the glass from my hand and took a sip. Setting the wine glass down, she eyed the plate of fresh oysters that sat on my desk. "What's that?"

"Oysters on the half shell. Tell me you've had them before."

She bit her bottom lip and looked up at me, shaking her head. "No. Never. How do you eat them?"

I walked over to where she stood and picked up one of the lemon slices, squirting it over one of the oysters. Then I gently loosened it with one of the cocktail forks and turned to her. "Close your eyes."

"Spencer..."

"Close your eyes," I repeated.

. . .

She looked at me but then did as she was told. I gently placed my hand on her lower back, her body tensing as it responded to my touch . Immediately, I felt a surge of excitement run through my body as my hand rested there.

"I'm going to bring the shell up to your mouth. I want you to part your lips and tilt your head slightly back. Allow the oyster to slide into your mouth, chew twice, and swallow."

She nodded. I brought the shell to her soft, full lips and tilted it to allow the oyster to slide off. I was lost as I watched the expression on her face as the oyster slid off the shell and into her mouth. I felt my cock harden as her tongue jutted out as she licked her lips then slowly opened her eyes.

Her eyes met mine, and for a moment, we were lost in each other's stare. Instead of leaning in and kissing her like I wanted, I smiled. "How was that?"

"Different," she said in a low, sultry voice.

. . .

"Want another?"

She studied my gaze then nodded. I repeated everything, only this time, I couldn't hold back. When she opened her eyes and gave me that heady gaze, I leaned in and took her mouth with mine. Immediately, she brought her arms up and rested them on my shoulders as her lips moved with mine. When I heard a soft moan escape her throat, I pulled her tightly into me, allowing her to feel how hard I was for her. I could feel her body start to let go, but then she placed her hands on my chest, breaking the kiss.

"I can't...we can't..." she said, breathless, looking up at me with watery eyes. "What about Nikki."

I didn't have a chance to say anything because she was already gone, having bolted from my office. I clenched my hands into fists and leaned onto my desk. Everything was a mess, and as I stood there trying to figure out how to explain to her that I didn't want us to be over, I heard the loud ding of the elevator. My heart sank as I stepped out into the hall just in time to see the elevator doors slide shut. She was gone.

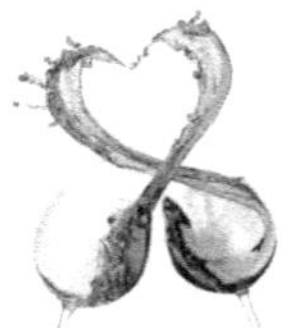

I spent Saturday morning clearing the driveway from the snow that had fallen the night before. I'd secretly hoped to see Ainsley, as she normally went out early on Saturday mornings for her yoga class, but she was nowhere to be found this morning. I wanted to talk to her, to apologize for last night. I'd left her messages, but she still hadn't read any of them.

I was putting the snowblower back in the garage when I heard my name. I turned to see Jon standing in my driveway. I was expecting Ainsley had talked to him about last night and he was here to blast me but was surprised when he smiled instead. "Hey, you feel like getting out for a beer tonight?" he questioned.

I wasn't sure where this was coming from. The man had not spoken to me in a couple of months, ever since he had caught us in bed.

"Sure. Where you want to go?"

. . .

"Just over to Darcy's. It's close. We don't have to worry about driving," he said.

"Sounds good."

"All right, meet you over there at five?" he asked.

"Great, in time for the game."

"Yep. See you then."

I'd hoped that his invitation meant that he was ready to forgive me and that it would give me an opportunity to explain to him how I truly felt about his daughter. I'd spent the afternoon running over what I wanted to say to him in my mind, and when I was sure I finally had everything down, I got ready. I made my way over to Darcy's and was surprised when I walked into the little neighborhood pub to see Jon already there, milking down a beer and digging into a plate of nachos.

. . .

"Hey," I said, sliding into the booth across from Jon.

"Hey, thought we'd watch the game?" Jon said. "You know, like old times."

"Yeah, sounds good."

I ordered a beer and then sat there watching the game, debating on when I should bring up the subject.

"What's new?" Jon asked, trying to break the awkward silence between us.

I shook my head. "Nothing. I really want to take a minute and talk to you about something," I bit out.

"About what?"

. . .

"I want to talk to you about Ain—"

Jon held up his hand, stopping me from saying anything more. "Spencer, I think out of respect for whatever friendship we might have left that we should just leave all that in the past. Let's just move forward and pretend that nothing happened okay. Ainsley is off-limits to you now, you know that, and once the new year hits, you will sign her transfer and allow her to move on with her life and job."

When he was finished, he looked right into my eyes. I could tell just from the glare that he was serious, then he turned his attention back to the TV, while I sat there holding my beer. All I wanted was to be able to express just how empty I felt without her in my life. Explain to him how much I loved her, but even if I did, I knew now that Jon would never approve of me dating his daughter, and that no matter how I felt about her, his opinion would probably never change.

Ainsley

Monday morning had arrived, and I knew that I could no longer hide out in my bedroom. The weekend had gone by in a blur, not because I'd been busy, but because I had spent the entire weekend in bed, thinking about that kiss. I had even missed my Saturday-morning yoga class. When I'd arrived home Friday night, I walked by my father, mumbling that I felt like I was coming down with the flu just so he wouldn't see the tears that had fallen on the way home.

I'd worried all the way into the office, white-knuckling it through traffic that I would have to face Spencer after running out on him on Friday night. Instead, his office door sat closed from the time I'd arrived. He was knee deep in phone meetings with some of his CEOs, and I couldn't have been happier.

I'd felt the weight lift off me as I left for lunch, and I now sat alone at a table in my favorite restaurant with a hot bowl of cheese ravioli in front of me and garlic bread smothered in cheese.

I scrolled through my phone at the messages that had come in over the weekend—three from Spencer and about fifteen from Carly. I hadn't spoken to her all weekend and decided I should probably return her messages. I dialed her number and smiled when I heard her pick up the phone.

"You're alive." She giggled.

"Yes, how are you?"

"Fine. Where the hell you been all weekend? I thought we were going to hang out."

I shoved a piece of ravioli in my mouth. "Sorry, I was sick."

The phone was quiet. "Are you all right?" Carly asked, concern lining her voice.

"Yeah. I've been working long hours, and Friday was more than I could handle. I guess it all just caught up with me."

"What did?"

"Spencer, all the feelings I still have."

"Ainsley."

"I know what you are going to say. I need to get over him, but I've wanted him for so long. You have no clue how I feel about him, and now not to be able to have him is just unbearable." My voice cracked and my throat burned as I held back tears.

"How many times do I need to tell you to let him go," Carly said, getting annoyed. "I told you he was too old for you in the first place and that you'd end up getting hurt. Besides, I thought you were putting in a transfer or a resignation."

"I did. He refused to sign the transfer."

"What? Why? How can he do that?"

"Because he can. He is the boss, remember. Besides, he can't train someone new at this time of year, and with the Christmas party needing to be organized, he would rather have someone experienced. A new person would just be totally overwhelmed."

"Ainsley, he has an events division. You aren't an event planner."

"Yes, however, the girl is off. She just had surgery, so he is helping me plan the event."

"Ainsley, can't you see what he is doing?"

I knew exactly what he was doing. He was doing exactly what I wanted him to do. I didn't want to work in another division of his company. I wanted to be as close to him as I could, only with everyone pushing against us, I couldn't let on that that was what I wanted. I certainly couldn't tell Carly about that kiss on Friday night and how it stirred emotions in me that I had hoped were dead.

"He's looking out for his company. I told him I would

stay and help only if he promised to sign the transfer in the new year."

"Uh huh, and what did he say?"

"He agreed."

The phone was silent for a moment. "You know, Ainsley, I think for your own good, you need to come away with me next weekend. There is someone I think you should meet, guaranteed to get Spencer off your mind. He's tall, handsome, funny, and most importantly...your age."

This was just like Carly, trying to persuade me to date someone else. She sounded just like my father. All I wanted was for one person to understand how I felt.

"What if I don't want to get my mind off of Spencer?"

"Ainsley, did something happen between you? What's got you all wrapped up in him again?" Carly questioned. "Last time I talked to you, I was sure you agreed it was over."

I debated not telling her, but she was my best friend, and the only one I could share this with. I let out a heavy sigh, playing Friday night over in my mind, my body filling with that tingling feeling I'd felt the moment he'd placed his hand on my lower back.

"He, um, he kissed me."

"Ainsley, are you serious."

"Yes, and, Carly, it was just as wonderful as I remembered."

"What happened?"

"At first, I kissed him back, but then I ran. All the feelings hit, and as much as I feel for him, I don't him to lose Nikki, and I don't want my father pissed off at me for the rest of my life."

"Your father loves you. He isn't going to be pissed off at you for the rest of your life."

"Carly, you have no idea how hard these past couple of months have been between us. He looks at me through disappointed eyes. He's finally speaking to me again the way he used to. If he were to find out, he would be livid all over again."

"Exactly how much time have you been spending at the office?" Carly asked.

"Almost every night of the week until eight or nine. There is a lot of planning to do for this event. I want to do a good job and make sure I don't mess up anything or miss something."

"I'm sure there is. Are you there working alone or are you there with him?"

"Spencer works all the time. Some nights he's there long after I leave, others he leaves when I do."

"I see, and over the last few weeks, how many times has he tried something?"

I rolled my eyes. "Only this once."

"I don't believe it. There has been no touching, no trying to make a pass at you, nothing."

I thought back to a few times I'd dodged him. An innocent touch on the arm, a lingering look, or a hand resting on my lower back as I walked through a door. That had been all, and I'd evaded them all, except for Friday night. It had been a moment of weakness on my part. I'd spent the better part of my day in my own head wishing that things were back to normal. I'd wanted him to pin me against the wall like he'd done before, to kiss me until I was utterly breathless, panting and begging for him to touch me more. Only when he had taken that step, I got scared. Scared at how I felt as his lips danced over mine. I'd run out of his office like a scared little girl, instead of allowing myself to succumb to those feelings.

"No, there has been nothing. He promised me he would be professional," I lied.

"I'm sorry, Ainsley, but I don't believe you," Carly said matter of fact.

I was about to roll my eyes when I looked up to see Spencer standing in front of me, a dozen red roses in his hand with a balloon that said “I'm sorry” floating in the air.

"Are you there?" Carly blurted into my ear, pulling me away from the man standing in front of me.

"Yes, sorry. Look, I have to run. It’s time to get back to the office. I have a meeting with the caterer in twenty minutes, and I need to set up the board room."

"Okay, but you better call me later on."

"I will."

I hung up the phone and looked at Spencer who held the flowers out for me to take. I reached out, gripping the bouquet, and brought them to my nose.

"In case you're wondering, they are because of Friday night. I'm sorry. I crossed a line. I hope you'll forgive me."

Spencer

The second snowstorm of the season raged outside, and I sat by the fire in my living room going over all the details for the event that Ainsley had put together. I looked over the spreadsheets, my mind running back to earlier today when she'd come into my office happy as ever that she'd struck a better deal with the hotel than she had originally. She was so happy and proud of herself, and I'd done only what I would naturally do: I hugged her and leaned in for a kiss. Only instead of expecting her to allow me to, she shoved me away and left my office in a huff. I had blown my apology to her in under two hours.

I shook my head, bringing me back to the present, and began looking over the invitation list. Some names were highlighted in green, others red, some yellow and orange. I had no idea what all that meant, even though Ainsley had gone over it with me three times today. I ran my hand over my face and picked up my phone and dialed Ainsley's number. After four rings, I knew she wasn't going to answer, so I went to old faithful in case she was with her father.

ROMANTICALPHA42: Are you busy?

Instantly, the three little dots danced on my screen.

BABYGIRL89: Perhaps. Why do you think I didn't answer my phone.

I smiled and quickly typed out another message.

ROMANTICALPHA42: Would you be able to pop by. I'm having issues with this spreadsheet for the invites.

BABYGIRL89: What kind of issues?

ROMANTICALPHA42: Guess you could say I'm just lost without you.

I knew there was a double meaning to that last text, and I'd hoped she'd picked up on it, but she didn't respond.

ROMANTICALPHA42: Think you could do me a favor and stop by?

I sat there waiting for a response for five minutes before I threw my phone down on the couch and blew out a breath. I threw my head back and slouched down on the couch, squeezing the bridge of my nose. I picked up my phone and looked at our texts. Still nothing. I was about to get up and drown my sorrows in a glass of scotch when I heard a knock on the door.

I jumped up, and walked over to the door, pulling it open. I was shocked to see Ainsley standing there, shivering, her arms crossed over her chest trying to keep herself warm.

"Sorry, had to wait for Dad to leave."

I glanced out at the dark road and pulled her inside. I watched as she slipped her shoes off and turned to look at me. "What help did you need?" she asked.

"Come with me," I said, allowing her to go first. "I'm working in the living room."

She walked in and stopped at the end of the coffee table and waited until I sat down, then she moved over beside me, close enough that her thigh touched mine.

I pointed to the screen, to the different colored names on the spreadsheet. Then she chuckled.

"I told you about this today. Red is a no, green is yes, orange and yellow are maybe and maybe with guest."

"Oh, that's right," I said, trying to play it up, but Ainsley wasn't having it.

"Spencer, I know you don't forget that easily. I also know that this was the same system your old assistant used because I was the one who found her notes. So what am I doing here."

I blew out a breath and looked down at the floor. Aside from the fact that I had barely heard a word she had said this afternoon because I couldn't stop imagining her under me, I really only had one more shot at trying to win her back.

"Ainsley, I'm done with everyone else making my decisions for me. I'm done with letting Brittany run my life for fear of her taking Nikki from me. I'm done with your father putting his foot down when he knows next to nothing about how I feel about you. I'm in love with you. No one needs to know or believe that but you, and it kills me when, every time I try to express that to you, you push me away, when I know from your body's responses that you feel the same way."

I turned and looked at her. Her eyes said everything, and I leaned forward and slowly brought my lips to hers. I braced myself for her to shove me away, but instead she surprised me by placing her hands on my neck and kissing me back.

As the kiss deepened, she hoisted herself up and straddled my lap, kissing me hard. Instantly, my cock hardened, and she ground herself down on me, a soft moan escaping her lips as I ran my hands down the side of her body, my thumbs running over her already hardened nipples.

"I want you," I murmured between kisses. "So bad."

"Then take me," she whispered back. "Please take me."

I secured my arm under her and stood up, carrying her down to my bedroom. I kicked the door shut and placed her gently down on the bed. She pulled her shirt off over her head, while I opened the button on her jeans. I was surprised to find she was wearing my favorite pair of black-and-pink panties, ones I'd gotten her for her birthday, and I leaned down and kissed her just above the waistband. Gripping the waist of her jeans, I inched them down her body, kissing her as I went.

By the time I'd made my way back up her body, she was panting, her eyes heady with want. I knelt before her and pulled my shirt off over my head then flicked the button open on my own jeans. She couldn't wait, and before I could object, she'd already pulled my cock from my pants and had started to stroke me.

I gripped her one ankle, biting gently into the calf of her leg before I ran my thumb over the crotch of her panties. They were already soaked, and I pressed just hard enough that she would feel me touching her through the silky fabric. She dropped back on the bed, letting go of my cock. I grabbed her other leg and slid her panties off, spreading her legs.

I could feel my own orgasm building as I ran my cock through her slick heat and pressed at her opening, sliding in slowly. She let out a soft moan, and I started to move inside of her as I held her close. She gripped my back, and wrapped her legs tightly around my waste. As bad as I wanted to reach this first release, I slowed our love making down and allowed myself to get lost in her, something I'd almost forgotten how to do.

When I felt her fingers dig into my back and her start to tighten around me I knew she was close. I wrapped my arms around her even tighter as she started to moan.

When she yelled out my name one final time, I felt myself let go and I poured myself into her.

Ainsley

As the days passed and Christmas crept closer, I started to regret handing in my transfer form. I'd regretted making that deal with Spencer. Things between us were back to normal. Over the last two weeks, I had come home late every night. Spencer and I had been busy making up for lost time while I continued lying to my father telling him that it was either work keeping me at the office late at night or I was busy with Carly.

I lay in bed looking up at the grey sky and snow-covered trees. It was a week before Christmas and the day of the party and I glanced at the clock. It was only nine. I didn't have to be at the hotel until at least three to go over and make sure everything was ready.

"Ainsley, are you getting up for breakfast?" Dad called from the hall.

"Be out in a few minutes," I called as my stomach turned at the thought of food.

"Good, because your eggs are getting cold."

I swallowed hard, trying to stop myself from being sick, but it did little good, and I bolted from the bed and into the bathroom just in time to be sick. I took a cloth and ran cool water over it, soaking it and then placing it on the back of my neck, when I heard a knock on the door.

"Ainsley, are you okay in there?"

"Yeah, Dad. I'm fine," I said, getting up off the floor and opening the door. "It's just nerves. I was feeling pretty off when I got home last night. All this planning for one day, I don't know how on earth these event planners do it."

"Ainsley, you're flushed," he said, bringing his hand up to my forehead. "You don't feel like you have a fever." He looked concerned as he reached into the medicine cabinet for the thermometer.

"I'm fine, seriously," I said, pushing past him and into my room.

"You've been overdoing it. I'll be happy once your transfer is completed. That way you will get your proper rest."

"Yeah, but just you wait and see the party. You are going to be so proud of me." I smiled.

"I'm sure I will be. Get dressed. I'll be in the kitchen,"

he said, taking another concerned look at me before turning to leave.

I threw on my favorite pair of jeans and sweatshirt and put my hair up into a high ponytail. Then I made my way to the kitchen for breakfast.

I'd been fine the rest of the day until they served dinner. I'd ordered the roast beef and as soon as the plate had been placed in front of me, my stomach turned. Spencer looked at me, concern lining his face as I excused myself from the table numerous times throughout the meal, barely touching any of my food. This last time had hit when they placed my favorite dessert, creme brule, in front of me. I'd taken one bite and couldn't even swallow. With my mouth full, I'd gotten up and excused myself from the table. Now, I sat on the floor huddled in front of the toilet in the washroom just off the ballroom, feeling like I could be sick again at any moment when I heard the door open.

"Ainsley, it's Kate. Are you all right, dear?"

"Yeah, I'm okay. I must be coming down with the flu," I answered. "Too many late nights working on this event."

"Oh dear. Spencer just wanted me to pop in and make sure you were all right. Do you need anything?" Kate was an older lady, the assistant to one of Spencer's executives. She sat at the desk next to me, and she knew how many late nights I'd been working. "Do you want some water? Ginger Ale, anything?"

"Maybe some motion sickness medication if you have it?"

"I do." I heard her unzip her clutch and slip two tablets under the stall door along with a little cup of water. "You know I always have those in my purse."

I giggled. Her purse was like a drugstore. "Thank you. I'll be out shortly. Let Spencer know I am fine."

"All right, dear."

I swallowed the two tablets she had given me, and, once the sick feeling passed, I stood up and opened the door. I stood in front of the mirror smoothing the material of the red dress I'd purchased just for tonight. Then I reapplied my lipstick and started on my way back to the party.

The plates had been cleared, music was playing, and people were up dancing. I glanced over to where Spencer stood. He looked amazing. He wore a perfectly fitted, perfectly pressed black suit, and he smiled as he stood there speaking with a couple of clients. I watched as he worked the room, moving from client to client, greeting them, talking to them, and then moving to the next. He was just about to approach another couple when he saw me. Instead of striking up a conversation with them, he greeted them and excused himself, letting them know he would be right back. I watched as he made his way over to me.

"Are you sure you're okay?" he asked, placing his hand on my lower back.

"Yes. I've just overdone it. Kate gave me a couple of her motion sickness tablets, so I should be okay now."

"You're sure?" He looked at me, concern still lining his face. "I can take you home."

"That's not necessary. Let's go and mingle, shall we," I said, smiling up at him and placing my arm through his.

We'd spoken to a few couples, and then we turned and headed for the dance floor for the first slow song of the evening.

"Care to dance?" he whispered in my ear.

"Love to. Probably wise to do so now before my father arrives. He said he would be here after work."

He gathered me in his arms. I rested my head on his chest and we danced together. Once the song was over, we turned to leave the dance floor to continue mingling when we both stopped in our tracks. My father had seen the entire dance. He stood there, glaring at us both. I'd been caught in the lie once again.

Spencer didn't even try to hide the fact that we were together. Instead, he took hold of my hand and he led me off the dance floor in the direction of my father.

"What are you doing?" I whispered as I felt the nauseous feeling strike again.

"I told you, I'm done hiding," he whispered back, looking directly at my father as he approached us, a look on his face I'd never seen before.

"Spencer, can I have a word with you," he said in a low tone.

Spencer nodded at my father and then looked at me, letting me know not to panic as he left my side and began to follow my father over to a quiet corner of the room.

"No, I want to speak to the pair of you."

Spencer

Ainsley held my hand tightly as we walked across the room following her father. I just prayed he wasn't going to have some sort of meltdown at the fact he'd caught me with his daughter again. I couldn't afford to have all of my clients witness this. I was surprised when he continued his way out of the room and into the hall, and I felt a weight lift off my shoulders at the fact that the drama wasn't actually going to happen in front of my clients.

Ainsley's hand started to shake as I allowed her to exit before me. Then she turned and looked at me, worry in her eyes. Jon had already walked across the hall and stood in front of one of the tables, watching us while he waited for us to join him.

I grabbed Ainsley's hand and stopped her from going ahead any farther. I pulled her into me and whispered in her ear, "If you'd prefer I talk to him on my own, that is fine."

She nodded. "I think that is best. I just can't bear to hear what he has to say."

I nodded and leaned in and placed a long kiss on her cheek and she turned to go back into the party when Jon cleared his throat. "Before you leave, Ainsley, give me a chance to speak to both of you. It's something you both should hear."

Ainsley turned and looked to me, completely unsure of what she should do.

"I've got you," I whispered to her as she hesitated. She looked to her father and back to me and then stepped up beside me and wrapped her arm around mine. Together we walked over to where Jon stood, Ainsley gripping my hand.

Jon looked at both of us, then down to where our hands were clasped together. I was prepared to be blasted and placed my arm around Ainsley's back, letting her know I had her.

"I think it's time that I apologize to the both of you," he said, looking to us.

I nodded, but Ainsley stood there, an unsure look on her face.

"I was wrong, Ainsley," Her Dad said looking to both of us. "Spencer, I was watching you guys tonight on the dancefloor. I can tell you care a great deal for my daughter."

"I do."

"Ainsley, I sometimes forget that you are a grown woman and not the five-year-old little girl you once were. I forget that you are capable of making your own choices, and even if I don't approve of them, they are still your choices and they should be respected. If they are wrong, well, they are your mistakes to live with."

"Spencer isn't wrong for me, Daddy. I'm in love with him," Ainsley said.

I gripped her tighter in my arm, pulling her against me.

"After watching you both tonight, I realize that now."

"Your daughter is in good hands, Jon."

"I know. I've seen how the two of you look at one another. I was a fool. I hope you both can forgive me."

I looked over at Ainsley and smiled, then held out my hand for her dad to shake. Then her Dad turned to Ainsley and held his arms open. She stepped forward and they hugged.

"You did a phenomenal job on this party. I'm so proud of you."

"Thanks. Does this mean I don't have to quit my job?" Ainsley asked him, and I chuckled to myself.

"That's up to Spencer," Jon said.

Ainsley turned and looked over her shoulder at me,

and I shrugged. "I've already submitted your transfer," I kidded.

"You did what?" she asked, looking at me shocked.

"I submitted it already...to my shredding bin."

Ainsley smiled at me and started to laugh, and then I heard my name inside the ballroom.

"That's my cue," I said, glancing at my watch. "You guys need to come inside. It's time for me to give my speech."

I took off in the opposite direction of Jon and Ainsley and made my way through the door that led to the back of the stage and walked out just in time to take the microphone. I looked out over the large crowd and finally spotted Ainsley standing off to the side with her dad.

"I want to thank each and every one of you for coming to this amazing Christmas party. As many of you know, I have spent the better part of last few years building this company from the ground up. What you don't know is why I started Finding Forever. You see, my older brother lost his wife after twenty-two years of marriage. After a few years, he started dating again. Friends tried to fix him up, he tried numerous online sites, and after watching these relationships fail over and over, I decided that there was something lacking with each of them. That is how Finding Forever was born, an elite site meant to match you to your forever partner using the power of psychology instead of an 'at first glance' approach.

“I am happy to say that, after all these years, we still hold a ninety-eight percent match rate. Which brings me to announce that even I decided to use my own company. This past summer I was fortunate enough to meet a young woman who awakened my soul."

I paused to take a drink and looked over to the side where Ainsley stood, her eyes wide as she waited for what was next. "You will know the young woman as Ainsley Matthews, my executive assistant and the woman in charge of putting this amazing party together. Ainsley, would you come up here for a moment please."

I looked down to where she stood, shaking her head, holding her hands over her mouth in shock, while her father walked her over to the stairs. Kate stood at the bottom of the stairs to help her up, and soon she was standing at my side.

It was after one when I pulled my car into my driveway. I glanced over at the passenger's seat to see Ainsley sound asleep. I cut the engine and placed my hand on her knee, shaking her gently.

"We're home," I whispered and watched her sleepy blue eyes open.

"What? Oh, I didn't mean to drift off," she said, gathering her items in a bit of a panic.

"Sweetie, relax," I said, leaning over and taking her purse from her hands. I climbed out of the car and walked around and opened her door, helping her out of the car. We walked slowly up the slippery walkway, and I slid my key in the lock. This was the first night that Ainsley would be spending the night with me, under my roof with her father's blessing.

I hung my suit jacket on the banister and guided Ainsley up the steps. I flipped the light on, lighting the twelve-foot tree that stood in the corner of living room. "Why don't you take a seat. I'll get us a glass of wine," I said, placing a kiss on her cheek.

"I think I'm going to change first."

"Sure, there are T-shirts in the top drawer in my room."

Ten minutes later, I sat in the living room, glass of wine in hand with soft Christmas music playing on the radio. Ainsley walked into the living room, looking sexy as hell in one of my T-shirts, her hair falling softly on her shoulders.

She sat down on the couch beside me, reaching for the glass of wine I'd poured for her, and took a sip. She closed her eyes as she swallowed and relaxed into the couch, placing her feet across my lap.

I set my glass down, grabbing her foot, rubbing it

gently in all the spots I knew she loved. A soft moan escaped her lips as I traveled up her calf. She looked at me, her eyes half asleep. I raised her leg and placed a kiss on her ankle, watching her response as I kissed my way up her calf. When I hit her knee, I reached for her wine glass, taking it from her hand, and placed it on the table beside mine.

"What...what are..."

I said nothing. I stood, slid one arm under her leg, the other behind her back, and lifted her off the couch and carried her down to the bedroom.

Ainsley

I was breathing hard when I woke up. I looked over to Spencer, who was uncovered to the waist, sound asleep. I wasn't sure what it was I had been dreaming about but I kicked the covers off and swung my legs around. I sat there for a moment in the darkness when my stomach started to turn. I covered my mouth, got up, and bolted to the bathroom.

Placing a cool cloth on the back of my neck, I rinsed my mouth with water and made my way to the living room where I curled up on the couch with my cell phone and called Carly. I could only imagine how irritated she would be for calling her so early, but I didn't care. I needed someone.

"Hey, sorry, I know it's early," I whispered into the phone.

"Ainsley, early? It's not even six. What is it? What's wrong?"

"I'm just not feeling well. I spent most of last night sick and again this morning."

"Is it nerves or the flu?"

"I don't know."

"Look, why don't you come over. We can go for breakfast, you can tell me all about the party."

I looked around the living room. I was sure Spencer would sleep in. "All right, I'll be there shortly."

I quickly ran home and slipped into my jeans and sweatshirt, climbed into my car, and headed to Carly's.

An hour later, we sat in the local diner waiting for our breakfast to be delivered.

"So, my father gave us his blessing," I said, looking at Carly for her reaction.

"You mean he is okay with you and Spencer?" she asked.

I nodded. "Yes. I am so happy, Carly, I can't even begin to tell you."

I could already tell from the look on Carly's face that she didn't approve of what my father had done, but she smiled anyways. "I'm happy to hear that. Are you feeling better now?"

I nodded, and then the server arrived holding our plates. "Pancakes and bacon for you," she said, sliding a plate in front of Carly, "and for you, eggs, bacon and toast.

Eggs over easy just the way you asked," she said, smiling, and then turned to walk away.

"This looks amazing," Carly said, digging into the steaming pile of pancakes. "I've been dying to come here for breakfast again."

I looked down at my plate, took one look at the eggs, and felt my stomach start to turn. I bolted from the table without a word and ran to the washroom. When I finally returned to the table, Carly sat there looking at me with a curious look on her face.

"So, yesterday you said you got sick at the party."

I nodded.

"What were you doing?"

"They brought out my dinner, and just like this morning, I had to run."

"I see," she said, nodding and looking at me with curiosity.

"What?" I questioned.

"I think we need to make a stop on the way home."

I looked at her, wondering where she wanted to stop. "Where?"

"The drugstore."

An hour later, we were back in Carly's room with her door locked. I looked over at my friend who stood there holding the bright-pink box out for me to take.

"No way, you are crazy. I'm telling you it's the flu," I said with my arms crossed.

"How many times have you had unprotected sex with him?" Carly urged.

I waved my hand, dismissing the idea, deep down inside praying that she didn't know what she was talking about. "It's the flu."

"Yes, okay, sure. It might be, but it's better to be safe than sorry. So get in there and take this," she said, waving the box in front of me.

I looked at my friend and shook my head. I knew she wasn't going to give up, so I took the box from her hand and slowly made my way into her bathroom. It was the longest three minutes I think I had ever lived as I stood in the bathroom looking down at that little white stick. I blinked hard as I saw the first little line appear, followed by a faint second line that got a little darker the longer I waited. I closed my eyes and let out a breath, looking back down at the little white stick, making sure that what I had seen was really there as my stomach started to turn for a completely different reason.

"Are you coming out or what?" I heard from the other side of the door. "It's been like five minutes."

I picked up the stick and turned to the door. I closed my eyes as I grabbed the handle and pulled the door open. Carly took one look at me and already knew what I was about to tell her.

"What are you going to do?" she asked, more panicked than I seemed.

"Um, well, I guess I need to tell Spencer," I said, shrugging.

"Today? Aren't you going to let it sink in or perhaps have it confirmed by a doctor first?" Carly questioned, following me around her room while I slipped into my coat.

I shook my head, picked up my purse, and slid the pregnancy test inside. "I'll call you later?" I said, turning to her.

She wrapped her arms around me, pulling me in for a hug, and then walked me to the door.

Spencer

I slowly opened my eyes and rolled over, reaching to the other side of the bed for Ainsley, but the bed was cold and empty. I sat up and looked around the room, listening hard to see if I could hear her in the kitchen, but the house was silent. I kicked the covers off me, picking my boxers up off the floor and slid them on.

I walked down the hall to the living room. The tree was on, soft Christmas music played. Ainsley was sound asleep, curled up on the couch, covered by a blanket. I smiled and walked over, sitting down beside her, placing my hand on her cheek.

"Morning, beautiful," I said in a low voice.

She took in a deep breath and then opened her eyes, looking up at me. She smiled gently, stretching her arms over her head. "Morning."

"Is everything all right?" I questioned. It wasn't like her to sleep in the living room when she spent the night with me. Normally, I would awaken to her curled into my side.

"Yes," she whispered. "Everything is fine."

"Good. It's just normally you don't sleep out here," I said, looking around the room. "Did you have a bad dream."

She shook her head and smiled. "No."

"Well, then, come back to bed and let me ravish you for a couple of hours," I said as I started to pull the covers off her only to be disappointed to find that she was already dressed.

"Can we talk for a minute?" she asked, her hand resting on my wrist.

I took one look at the expression on her face and became rather concerned that something was wrong. I was instantly worried that she had changed her mind about us and started to prepare myself for the worst. "Sure."

She reached down beside the couch and picked up her purse. Opening it slowly, she reached inside and then looked at me. "I don't even know where to begin," she said, closing her eyes and taking in a breath.

"Well, you just say it," I said, smiling at her. "Our relationship will always be better if we are open with one another from the start."

She nodded and placed a pregnancy test in my hand. I looked down at it and then up to her, my eyes moving back down to those two little pink lines. I knew exactly what those meant, thinking back to when Brittany had told me about Nikki. I felt a twinge of excitement run through me.

"Okay," I said, trying hard not to show how I really felt because I wasn't sure how she was going to react.

"Okay, is that all you can say?"

I nodded. "What's going through your mind?" I questioned.

"Um, I'm scared."

"Why?"

I watched as she lay back against the couch. "Because I don't have any idea how you feel about this. You are much older than I. I have no idea if you want to be a father again."

"Well, one thing I can tell you is that Nikki is going to be so excited to find out she could have a little brother or sister, and honestly I feel the same way."

"You're excited that you could have a little brother or sister?"

I couldn't help but laugh. "No, silly."

"Then what?"

I looked at her, at the panic that lined her face, leaned down and kissed her softly. "I'm a little shocked, but ecstatic all at the same time. Ainsley, I'm in love with you. Nothing could change that."

"Really?"

"Really. Now I think that we need to head on down to my bedroom and spend some time celebrating, then we should make an appointment with your doctor. Then I will take the pleasure of telling your father."

"Oh God, do we have to tell him?" she asked, looking even more worried than she had moments before.

"Yes, we have to tell him. We have to tell Brittany too. Then after that, we are going to go shopping."

"Shopping?"

"Yes, we will need some baby things. A crib, change table, diapers, and clothes. However, one thing I know for a fact that we are going to need is already under the tree over there," I said, nodding to the tree.

I watched as she frowned and turned to look over at the tree. There was a pile of gifts under the tree that I'd had Ainsley personally wrap for Nikki at the office one night because Nikki had been staying with me and had been on a kick to find what Santa had gotten her.

I stood up and walked over to the tree, pulling a box out from under it. Then I walked back over, sat down, and pulled at the paper.

"I was going to give you this Christmas morning, but now is as good a time as any."

She lay there propped up on her elbow watching as I opened the package, dropping the gold paper on the table.

"Close your eyes."

She did as I asked, and I opened the box, holding it in my hand. "Go ahead, open them."

Her eyes met mine and then fell to my hand where inside that box sat an engagement ring. I couldn't help but chuckle as shock lined her face. I could tell she had no clue that this was coming, and so I took the ring I'd purchased two months earlier from the box, grabbed her hand, and slowly slid the ring onto her finger.

"Ainsley, I've known for a long time how I've felt about you. I also know what it's like not to have you, and I can say that I would rather have you at my side forever than not have you at all. Ainsley, will you be my forever?"

I watched as a tear slipped from her eye and ran down her cheek. She quickly wiped it away and looked at me, her eyes full of tears, and nodded. She wrapped her arms tightly around me. "Yes. Yes," she whispered.

She looked into my eyes. "Now we need to plan the wedding and tell my father," she said, looking a little worried.

I smiled and shook my head. "One thing at a time. I promise we will tell your father together, and we will hire someone to do all the wedding arrangements. However, first, we need to go and celebrate."

"What?"

I said nothing more. I stood up, slipped my arms under her body, picking her up off the couch, and kissed her as I carried her on down the hall. I could not wait to start this new chapter in my life with my soon to be wife.

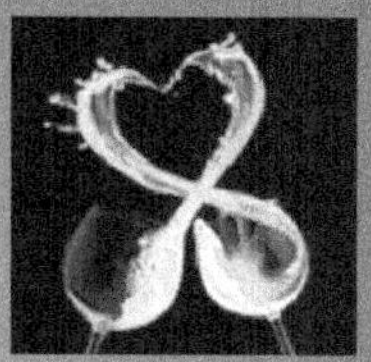

Coming Soon

What is coming next from S.L. Sterling

Willow Valley Series
A Small-Town Contemporary Romance Series

Memories of the Past
Releasing October 11
Preorder Today

The Holiday Dilemma
Releasing December 13
Preorder Today

About the Author

USA Today Bestselling Author S.L. Sterling was born and raised in southern Ontario. She now lives in Northern Ontario Canada and is married to her best friend and soul mate and their two dogs.

An avid reader all her life, S.L. Sterling dreamt of becoming an author. She decided to give writing a try after one of her favorite authors launched a course on how to write your novel. This course gave her the push she needed to put pen to paper and her debut novel "It Was Always You" was born.

When S.L. Sterling isn't writing or plotting her next novel she can be found curled up with a cup of coffee, blanket and the newest romance novel from one of her favorite authors.

In her spare time, she enjoys camping, hiking, sunny destinations, spending quality time with family and friends and of course reading.

Want to keep up to date with me. I invite you to join my weekly Newsletter.

If you love reader groups, come and join me in the Sterling's Silver Sapphires

Or, if you just prefer to check out my books you can visit my website.

Other Titles by S.L. Sterling

It Was Always You

On A Silent Night

Bad Company

Back to You this Christmas

Fireside Love

Holiday Wishes

Saviour Boy

The Boy Under the Gazebo

The Greatest Gift

Into the Sunset

Our Little Secret

The Malone Brother Series

A Kiss Beneath the Stars

In Your Arms

His to Hold

Finding Forever with You

Vegas MMA

Dagger

Doctors of Eastport General

Doctor Desire

All I Want for Christmas (Contemporary Romance Holiday Collection)

Constraint (KB Worlds: Everyday Heroes)

www.ingramcontent.com/pod-product-compliance
Lightning Source LLC
Jackson TN
JSHW022139140425
82609JS00005B/40

* 9 7 8 1 9 8 9 5 6 6 3 6 7 *